This igloo book belongs to:

....

D0352228

igloobooks

Published in 2020
by Igloo Books Ltd
Cottage Farm
Sywell
NN6 0BJ
www.igloobooks.com

Copyright © 2013 Igloo Books Ltd

Igloo Books is an imprint of Bonnier Books UK

All rights reserved. No part of this publication may be
reproduced or transmitted in any form or by any means,
electronic, or mechanical, including photocopying, recording,
or by any information storage and retrieval system,
without permission in writing from the publisher.
The measurements used are approximate.

0120 003
4 6 8 10 11 9 7 5
ISBN 978-1-78197-464-3

Written by Melanie Joyce
Illustrated by Mike Byrne
Printed and manufactured in China

My Grandad and Me

igloobooks

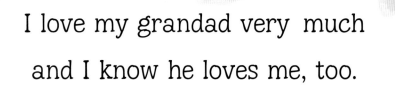

I love my grandad very much
and I know he loves me, too.

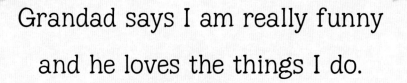

Grandad says I am really funny
and he loves the things I do.

I love my grandad because he's fun and I think of him every day.
That's why I get so excited when I go to his house to stay.

When I go to stay at Grandad's house,
I like to take all my things.
"Hello," he says, opening the door,
when the doorbell rings.

Grandad chuckles when he sees my case, my toys and my best teddy.
"Come in," he says with a great, big smile, "I've got a nice treat ready."

Me and Grandad go on adventures, to see what we can find.
Grandad always leads the way and I run along behind.

Grandad teaches me about the animals that live outside.

We look for bugs and beetles and find the places they hide.

Grandad loves me because I like things
that wriggle, squiggle and squirm.
"Let's take one home for Mummy,"
I say, when I find a big, fat, juicy worm.

Grandad laughs and says, "That would give Mummy a scare.
Let's pick her flowers instead, there are pretty ones over there."

When we stop for lunch, Grandad opens his big rucksack.

He always brings yummy treats for us in his red lunchpack.

Sometimes, I tell Grandad stories and I try to make them scary.
He loves the one about the monster who's purple, huge and hairy.

Grandad and me play at pirates and we look for chests packed full of gold.

He always gets to be the pirate captain, because he's very old.

We sail off to desert islands and ride the ocean waves.

We fight off other pirates and we're really very brave.

My grandad knows how to make me laugh when I am hurt or feeling sad.
"Come on," he says, pulling a funny face, "I'm sure things aren't that bad."

When I am feeling bored, Grandad says, "I know just the thing."

He takes me into the garden and pushes me, whoosh, on the swing.

Grandad loves me because I paint pictures of Dad and Mummy, too.

I paint a special picture for him and say, "Look, Grandad, it's you!"

Grandad says that if I eat my greens,
I'll grow up to be big and strong.

He looks at me with
tears in his eyes and says,
"It won't be long."

Grandad loves being outside with me, even in rainy weather.

We play at dodging raindrops and splash in puddles together.

I love it when the sun comes out and there's a rainbow in the sky, but the best bit is when we are back inside, all cosy, warm and dry.

Sometimes I have bad dreams and wake up in the night.

"Don't be afraid," says Grandad. "I'll switch on your night light."

Grandad finds my special story and he tucks me back into bed.

His voice makes me feel safe as he says, "Goodnight, Sleepyhead."

I really love my grandad because he is better than all the rest.
I know that my grandad is special, because he loves me the best.